THE LOST TREASURE

BY ELLIS BYRD

Penguin Young Readers Licenses
An Imprint of Penguin Random House

PENGUIN YOUNG READERS LICENSES
An Imprint of Penguin Random House LLC

Cover illustrated by Karianne Koski Hutchinson

ISBN 9780451534507   10 9 8 7 6 5 4 3 2 1

CHAPTER ONE

The salty sea breeze ruffled Peck's fur, causing the bell at the end of one of her long ears to jingle. The bunny Alpha gripped the railing of the ship and gazed at the endless sea stretching out before her, barely able to contain her excitement.

"I can see why Liza loves exploring," she told Cosmo, who stood at her side. "Who knows what we might find out there? The land on that map could be anything!"

"I know!" Cosmo grinned. "Think of all the new plants we might discover—and all the stories they'll have!" The koala Alpha had a deep understanding of the plants of Jamaa and often communicated with them.

"Tons, I bet!" Peck agreed. "And other surprises, too . . ."

"Do you really think there's some sort of treasure?"

"Of course!" Peck hopped up and down. "That's what happens when mysterious maps are involved. Maps *always* lead to treasure—and the real treasure is never what you expect! Maybe it'll be something I can use in my next art project . . . Oh, or maybe we'll discover a new musical instrument!"

Over at the helm, Liza smiled as she

gripped the wheel of the *Wayfarer*. Graham had designed the ship himself, and his team of builders now made up the crew. On deck, around a dozen monkeys, pandas, and foxes manned the sails, tugging on ropes and adjusting pulleys. Belowdecks, Graham and a smaller crew of otters were checking the hull and making sure the ship was operating smoothly. Unlike Peck and Cosmo, the monkey Alpha had little interest in a possible treasure or in exploring the unknown. In fact, when Liza first showed her fellow Alphas the map, Graham was the only one who'd shown no desire at all to sail the high seas.

"Adventure is all well and good, but we might also be putting ourselves in unnecessary danger," he'd pointed out. "If the fiasco at the Winter Games taught us anything, it's that Phantoms could be lurking anywhere."

"But that was months ago," Liza had replied. "There haven't been any signs of Phantom activity since then. And I believe it's our duty as Alphas to find this long-forgotten land."

"Furthermore," Sir Gilbert had added, eyes twinkling as he turned to Graham, "if we're to make this voyage, we will need someone to build a seaworthy ship."

Once Sir Gilbert said that, Graham had needed no further convincing. The challenge of designing and constructing a ship that could carry the Alphas and their animal friends across the sea was too great an opportunity for him to pass up.

And the *Wayfarer* was a beautiful ship, Liza thought, admiring the great white sails and gleaming beams of polished oak and cedar. The sun shone brightly down as they sailed over the sparkling blue water. But despite the gorgeous scenery, Liza's mind kept wandering back to the map rolled up in the wooden tube attached to her belt.

She'd discovered the map in the Forgotten Archive, an ancient library and repository filled with scrolls, books, and records from Jamaa's history. Liza had been doing research on the forgotten lands of Jamaa, poring over archaic texts and daydreaming about how exciting it would be to explore uncharted places. The panda Alpha had been so caught up in the idea that when she slid a particularly thick book back onto its shelf, the corner of yellowed paper sticking out of a thin crack had almost escaped her notice.

"That's odd." Carefully, Liza had pressed her paw to the wood. To her amazement, a secret compartment creaked open. An old map was folded inside, held in place by a shiny purple stone the likes of which Liza had never seen. One look at the map, and Liza's explorer instincts kicked in, and her heart had fluttered with excitement.

The map showed a large island shaped a little bit like a teardrop. Jagged triangles over the southern tip indicated rocky terrain, while the northern terrain was covered in tiny dots, which Liza knew meant sand. The middle of the island featured an intricate system of caves and wild jungle, and right in the heart of it all was a large X.

"X marks the spot, right, Liza?" Peck called, as if she'd read Liza's mind. "You think there's treasure, too, don't you?"

Liza laughed, turning the massive wheel slightly to the right to adjust their course. "I suppose it's possible!" she called back. "Right now, I'm too engrossed in how beautifully the *Wayfarer* is sailing to spare much thought for gold."

"I don't care about gold, either," Peck said, wrinkling her nose. "But I bet the treasure will be way more interesting than that."

Sir Gilbert, the tiger Alpha, stood at the bow of the ship, watching the waves crest against the hull. He too hoped Liza's map was leading them to something greater than gold: With any luck, they would discover lost Heartstones that had been stolen by the Phantoms years and years ago and never recovered. If they could return any Heartstones they found to Jamaa, new animal species would be able to live there.

Turning, Sir Gilbert squinted up at the crow's nest in the mainmast, where Greely was on lookout duty. "Any sign of land yet?"

The wolf Alpha didn't take his gaze off the horizon. "No," he replied shortly. Greely had no interest in treasure of any sort. However, discovering new land meant obtaining new knowledge, and that was an opportunity Greely would never turn down. He would have preferred doing so alone, but sailing the *Wayfarer* required a large crew. Once they reached land, Greely intended to explore in solitude. The other Alphas would have to be okay with that—they should have long ago accepted that he worked best this way, anyway.

The wind picked up, whipping Greely's purple cloak against his back. He frowned, his eyes locking onto a dark spot in the distance. Was it land? Greely started to call down to Liza, but some instinct caused him to hesitate. His fur stood on end, as if the wind carried static electricity. He squinted at the dark spot, which was growing larger by the second. A tiny flash caught his eye, quickly followed by another, and Greely realized the dark spot wasn't land at all.

"All hands on deck!"

"What's going on?" Liza called, looking up in alarm.

Greely grimaced as the *Wayfarer* sped toward the churning black clouds. Lightning flashed again, and this time, it was accompanied by the distant boom of thunder.

"A storm is coming!"

CHAPTER TWO

Graham was just finishing his inspection of the rudders when the ship lurched. Dropping his wrench, he stumbled and bumped into the wall.

"What's going on?" exclaimed Eugenie, an otter who had been assisting with the inspection. Overhead, Liza's commanding voice rose above the shouts and cries of the crew on deck.

"Batten down the hatches!"

A deafening crack of thunder sounded, and Graham hurried to the ladder.

"It's a storm!" he called to Eugenie. "We need to grab as many life jackets as we can!"

They scurried up to the deck, and Eugenie gasped. The sky, which had been cloudless and blue earlier, was now a strange, smoggy gray swirled with purple. Lightning flashed every few seconds, briefly casting a greenish glow on the churning water. A flash of lightning was followed by a great splintering crack, and Sir Gilbert sprinted across the deck.

"The mainsail!" he bellowed, grabbing the mast with both paws. "If we lose it, we won't be able to control the ship!"

Greely and several pandas joined him, pulling on the ropes holding the sail to the mast. Cosmo was tightening Liza's life jacket as she fought for control of the wheel—and then the mast snapped.

Liza watched as the wind carried the mast up and away, the mainsail and ropes tangled around it. The wheel went slack in her paws, and her eyes scanned the water ahead. There, barely visible through the storm, was the outline of a beach with palm trees blowing in the wind—an island!

"Land ahead!" she shouted, letting go of the wheel. "Abandon ship!"

The *Wayfarer* began to spin out of control. Liza hurried over to Cosmo and another koala, who were hurrying crew members onto the ship's lifeboats. Each time a boat was full, Greely would quickly lower it down into the water.

"Head for the beach!" Liza called as

the second-to-last lifeboat was carried off by the choppy waves. "We'll wait out the storm there!"

Peck and Graham jumped into the last lifeboat hanging on the side of the ship, and then helped Eugenie in. Sir Gilbert followed, grabbing the oars.

"Wait!" Cosmo cried, and Liza and Greely whirled around. One of the ropes had come loose, and the end was tied around another koala's leg. "Wylie's stuck!"

"Wylie!" Liza exclaimed as she hurried over. "How did this happen?"

"I didn't see it there," Wylie said, tugging frantically. "I must have stepped in the knot, and now it's too tight!"

"We're about to have a much bigger problem," Greely said, pointing. The other Alphas turned to look, and Peck gasped.

An enormous tidal wave was rising up in the distance. Without hesitating, Greely sliced the ropes holding the last lifeboat.

"Wait!" Sir Gilbert let out a roar of frustration as he, Peck, Graham, and Eugenie dropped safely onto the water.

"Get to shore!" Greely called down to them. "We'll meet you there!"

Any response from the tiger Alpha was lost to the wind. Turning back around, Greely noticed a loose plank sticking up out of the deck. He tugged it out just as Liza and Cosmo succeeded in freeing Wylie from the rope. Liza took one look at the plank and understood. "It's no lifeboat, but it will have to do!"

Together, the four animals hurried to the railing. But the ship began tipping up, sending them skidding and sliding from the bow down to the stern.

"We'll just have to jump from here!" Liza said. "One, two . . . three!"

They leaped off the *Wayfarer*, landing with a heavy splash. The great ship was almost vertical now, and they kicked hard, propelling their makeshift lifeboat out of the path of the tidal wave.

"The others went that way!" Cosmo cried, but it was no use. The massive wave crashed down, and the current beneath it was too strong to swim against. Liza, Cosmo, Greely, and Wylie clung to their small piece of the *Wayfarer* as the current whisked them far, far away from the beach . . . and their friends.

CHAPTER THREE

Sir Gilbert stood on the beach, watching as the sun began to peek out from the clouds. The *Wayfarer* lay on its side in the shallow water, its masts broken or missing completely. Dozens of crew members scurried over the fallen ship, securing it in place with ropes and anchors.

Now that the storm was clearing up, Sir Gilbert could appreciate how beautiful this island was: sparkling white sand, turquoise water, palm trees, bright pink and yellow flowers. Beyond the palm trees, the jungle was thick and dark, and Sir Gilbert half expected to see Liza and the others emerge at any moment. Surely they had washed up farther down the coast, he told himself. They couldn't be far.

"Sir Gilbert! Look!"

The tiger Alpha turned to see Peck splashing through the water toward him, waving a wooden tube over her head.

"Liza's map!" Sir Gilbert exclaimed. "Where did you find that?"

"Floating in the water over there." Peck pointed to the left of the *Wayfarer*. Her purple eyes were bright with worry. "But other than this, there's no sign of them. Do you think they're okay?"

"Of course," Sir Gilbert said, and he

meant it. "Greely, Liza, and Cosmo have been in more difficult situations, and they always come through. Wylie is perfectly safe with them."

Peck relaxed a bit. "Yeah, you're right."

Graham hopped off one of the *Wayfarer's* fallen beams and made his way toward them, Eugenie right behind him.

"Just finished our assessment of the damage," Graham announced when he reached his fellow Alphas. "It's bad, quite bad—but fixable, of course! All we need are supplies: something to sew up the ripped sails, nuts and bolts, and washers to hold them in place . . ."

"But we're stranded on a deserted island!" Peck exclaimed. "We can't get any of those things!"

Graham laughed. "Why, there's a jungle

full of potential gadgets and gizmos right over there. With a little creativity, I bet we can put together everything we need." His smile faded. "What about the others, though? Shouldn't we find them first?"

Sir Gilbert considered this. "Liza knew our lifeboats were headed for this beach," he said at last, gazing out at the wrecked ship. "She's an experienced explorer—she's likely leading them this way as we speak."

"So the best thing for us to do is stay put and fix the ship," Peck concluded. "We can get one of the crew members to look out for Liza and the others while we search the jungle for tools."

"We'll need other supplies, too," Eugenie piped up. "Fresh water, for one thing. And we lost a lot of food overboard."

Sir Gilbert nodded approvingly. "A fine point. Why don't you assign a lookout, Graham? In the meantime, Peck and I can search for food and water while you and Eugenie look for . . ." He paused, brow furrowed. "Just what will you be looking for, precisely?"

"No idea!" The monkey Alpha laughed, snapping his goggles on top of his head. "That's all part of the fun!" He waved before heading back to the *Wayfarer* with Eugenie.

Smiling, Sir Gilbert began making his way to the jungle. Peck hopped along at his side, pulling out the map as she did.

"You know, if I hold the map this way," she said, turning the paper sideways, "that beach kind of looks like *this* beach. See here, all those trees? Just like this jungle?"

Sir Gilbert squinted at the map. "Hmm. Do you think this is, in fact, the island we were searching for?"

"Maybe!" Peck said excitedly. "Liza said we were close, but I guess she didn't realize *how* close. Oh, I can't wait to tell her!"

The jungle was filled with plants and flowers unlike any Sir Gilbert had ever seen: giant red flowers that drooped like bells, and round yellow bulbs covered in spikes. One tree's branches were dotted with little purple orbs that tasted like grapes, and Sir Gilbert filled his bag with as many as he could.

Peck's nose was buried in the map as they walked. "I really think this is the island, Sir Gilbert!" she said when they reached a narrow river. "Look here, we're right at the blue squiggle!"

Sir Gilbert lowered his canteen into the river, scooping up the fresh water. "That would be most fortuitous." He gazed down the river. "Look at the size of those lily pads . . . They're absolutely enormous. I'm sure Graham will think of some way to put them to good use, don't you agree? Peck? Peck, are you listening to me?"

"What? Oh!" Blinking, Peck lowered the map. "Sorry. It's just that I think we're close to the path that leads to the X that marks the buried treasure! It's not too far from here, just up that way . . ."

Sir Gilbert arched a brow. "The buried treasure? Peck, it's quite exciting that we might be shipwrecked on the very island we were searching for. But right now, we are on a mission for supplies, not treasure. Perhaps we might use the map to find food, and—"

"We will, absolutely!" Peck was already scurrying down the riverbank. "I just want to check and see if I'm right!"

She veered left when the river curved right, plunging through bright green bushes. "The path's right on the other side of this patch of sand!" she called over her shoulder to Sir Gilbert. "It heads north, and . . . *ack!*"

Sir Gilbert emerged from the bushes to find Peck waist-deep in the ground, holding the map high over her head. All of Peck's instincts told her to wriggle and squirm, but every movement only made her sink another inch.

"It's quicksand!" Sir Gilbert said.

"Don't move, Peck. Wiggling will only make you sink faster."

"Ah." Peck stopped moving. She could still feel herself sinking, but much slower now. It took every bit of willpower she had not to struggle against the quicksand.

Sir Gilbert grabbed a stick and held it out to her, standing at the edge of the quicksand. Slowly, carefully, she reached for the stick . . . but it was too far away. Desperate, Peck lunged forward and felt herself sink another few inches.

"Stop!" Sir Gilbert cried, withdrawing the stick. "I'll find something longer."

He disappeared into the bushes. Peck held as still as possible, her heart pounding in her ears. She sank deeper, her body tilting sideways. Without thinking about it, she lowered her left arm to balance herself, plunging it into the quicksand.

"Oh, *Peck*," the bunny Alpha muttered. "Bad move."

Now just her head and right arm were above the quicksand. She tried tugging her left arm up, but when she felt the thick, grimy sand creeping up her neck, she froze. A moment later, Sir Gilbert reappeared holding a long, thick vine.

"I'm going to toss this to you," he said. "It's vital that you catch it on the first try— otherwise, your movement might cause you to sink entirely."

Peck swallowed hard. "I can't! My left arm is stuck, and I've got this." She waved her right paw, which was clutching the map.

Sir Gilbert's expression was grave. "Peck, you have to drop the map."

"No!" Peck thought frantically. "I'll . . .
I'll catch the vine with my teeth!"

"That's too risky. Just—"

"I can do it! Trust me!"

The quicksand was now up to her
chin. Grimacing, Sir Gilbert hesitated for a
moment. Then he tossed the vine out.

Peck lurched up, her jaw clamping
around the vine. "*Uhguhdih!*" she cried
triumphantly, and Sir Gilbert pulled the
vine as hard as he could. Peck rose up
slowly, slowly, and then:

Slorp!

The bunny Alpha went flying out of
the quicksand. She shrieked as she soared
directly toward Sir Gilbert, who barely had
time to drop the vine.

"*Oof!*" Peck slammed into Sir Gilbert
with surprising force, and they both

toppled to the ground. Rubbing her head, Peck slowly got to her feet. Then she noticed Sir Gilbert and burst into giggles.

The tiger Alpha's cloak covered his head, and his legs were tangled in the vine. He tried swiping the cloak out of his eyes, but only succeeded in tugging it farther down.

"Here, hold still." Peck scurried over and flipped the cloak over Sir Gilbert's head.

"Thank you," Sir Gilbert said, standing up with as much dignity as he could muster. Peck stifled her laughter as the tiger Alpha untangled the vine from his legs.

"Thank *you*," she said, glancing back at the quicksand. "I never would've forgiven myself if I'd lost the map."

"The map," Sir Gilbert repeated, sighing. "Peck, why are you more concerned with that map than your own safety?"

"I'm not, don't be silly!" Peck clutched the map to her chest. "It just would've been a terrible waste. We'd never find the treasure!"

Sir Gilbert studied his friend carefully. "I must ask . . . Why do you care so much about treasure? Could gold really mean that much to you?"

Peck blushed. "No, not gold," she told him, folding the map carefully. "Someone buried something and marked it on this map—so they must have wanted someone to find it! It's like a secret someone hid . . . just for us!"

"Well, I suppose I can understand that,"

Sir Gilbert said, smiling. "But let's not worry about treasure just yet, shall we? Not when we have a ship to repair and lost friends to find."

Peck nodded vigorously. "You're right," she agreed. But as they headed back to the river, she couldn't help casting a longing look at the path on the other side of the quicksand: the path that led to the *X*, and whatever mysterious treasure was buried there.

"These lily pads are incredible!"

Eugenie splashed into the river, swimming back to the riverbank where Graham stood waiting. "Are they as thick as they look?" he asked eagerly.

"Thicker!" Eugenie replied. "I bet one

of those lily pads could hold two rhinos without sinking!"

Graham clapped and laughed. "Perfect! Looks like we've found our new sails. We'll just have to bring a few crew members back here to help us haul them to the ship."

The two animals followed the river upstream, chatting enthusiastically as they kept an eye out for more potential tools and ship-building materials. Graham greatly enjoyed the otter's company. He was surprised to learn that she was very interested in architecture, and she had a creative way of looking at problems that Graham respected. He valued his fellow Alphas and appreciated their unique skills, but it was refreshing to spend time with someone so similar to himself. He was telling her the details of his latest invention back home, a purifier that separated dirt and grime from water so that it was clean to drink, when Eugenie gasped.

"Oh, look at that plant!"

She pointed to a bush the size of an elephant. Its leaves were extraordinarily long and wispy, bursting up from the center and then drooping over to graze the ground. Graham and Eugenie hurried over to examine the leaves.

"They seem really strong, despite how thin they are," Eugenie said, pulling one taut to demonstrate. "Graham, do you think we could use these as thread for sewing our new sails?"

Graham was impressed with her ingenuity. "Brilliant idea!" he said, and Eugenie blushed. They gathered dozens of the string-like leaves, wrapping them into coils so they wouldn't get knotted up inside Graham's bag. When they had finished, they continued their trek along the river. Graham and Eugenie both spotted the tree at the same time: a thick trunk covered with ivy and sharp spikes. Up close, they saw that the spikes had sharp, pointed ends.

Graham raised his eyebrows at Eugenie. "Are you thinking what I'm thinking?"

Eugenie grinned. "Needles!"

"Exactly!"

Graham felt pleased as they plucked out several spikes and placed them in his bag. With their makeshift needles and thread, along with those glorious lily pads, they were well on their way to rebuilding the *Wayfarer*. His mind was already racing, imagining the ways he could improve the ship to make it sail even faster.

"Let's take these materials to the *Wayfarer*," he told Eugenie. "Then we can bring back a few crew members to help us with those lily pads."

They retraced their steps down the riverbank and into the jungle. But after only a few minutes, a strange noise stopped them in their tracks. A rustling sound, accompanied by whispers, was coming from high overhead.

Graham and Eugenie looked up at the canopy of trees blocking the sky. The thick, bright green vines were wrapped around one another, forming a net. Tiny webbed paws poked through here and there, and Graham spotted several pairs of eyes blinking down at him.

Eugenie gasped. "The other otters from the *Wayfarer*!"

"Graham! Eugenie!" one cried. "Thank goodness you found us!"

"We wanted to come help you find supplies," another added. "But this net was under the grass, and it trapped us!"

"The vines are really thick," a third called down. "Even a sword probably couldn't cut these knots."

"Fascinating!" Graham exclaimed, and Eugenie elbowed him. "Er, I mean terrible. Terribly fascinating. Don't worry, we'll get you down from there!" He was already looking around at their surroundings.

"You're going to invent something, aren't you?" Eugenie asked eagerly. "How can I help?"

Graham didn't respond at first. His mind was working quickly, assessing the problem and the available resources he could use to come up with a solution. Then he snapped his fingers and beamed at Eugenie.

"I've got it!" he cried, holding out his bag. "Here, take out all the needles we've got, and thread one with one of those string leaves. I'll be right back."

Graham was a blur of motion, flitting back and forth between trees, looking for the strongest piece of bark he could find. He returned to Eugenie, and they set to work with the makeshift needle and thread. When they had finished, Graham held up the piece of bark. A row of sharp, tiny needles jutted out along the edge.

Eugenie beamed. "A saw!"

"Exactly!" Graham said, pleased. "Now, let's see if it's sharp enough . . ."

The monkey Alpha clambered up the tree closest to the net with the trapped otters. From the highest branch, he could see how the net was tied to the tree, stretching across the clearing to another tree. The knot was tight, the vine every bit as thick and strong as the otters had claimed.

Graham set to work with his new saw. After a minute, it was obvious the needles were sharp enough for the job. "Get ready to jump!" Graham called to the otters as the vine started to fray. "One, two . . . three!" The vine snapped, and the net fell.

"We're free!" one of the otters cried, leaping onto a branch along with his friends. Graham and the otters climbed down and hurried over to Eugenie. When the last otter joined them, Eugenie gasped.

"Did the vines hurt your eye?"

The otter touched the black eye patch covering his right eye. "Oh, no! I found this on the beach and put it on for fun."

Eugenie and the other otters laughed.

"You look like a pirate," one said.

"*Arrr*, matey," another joked.

"Well, my pirate friends," Graham said with a smile. "Care to help us carry a few giant lily pads back to the *Wayfarer*?"

"Aye, aye!" they cried, and Eugenie led the way back to the river. Graham picked up his bag and followed, laughing along with the others. But he couldn't help wondering about the eye patch. Whoever had worn it had no doubt been the one to set that trap with the net.

Graham thought of his missing friends, and his brow furrowed with worry. Apparently this island wasn't as deserted as it appeared.

CHAPTER FOUR

Cosmo reached between two jagged rocks, carefully pulling out a strand of bright green seaweed. "What's that now?" He tilted his head, listening hard to the briny plant. Then he stood up quickly, squinting at the massive boulders a little farther inland. Movement caught his eye on one of the smaller rocks nearby.

"Wylie!" he called, and the koala glanced over his shoulder.

"Yes?"

"Where's Liza?" Cosmo asked eagerly, still clutching the seaweed as he joined Wylie. "My friend here has just given me some information I think she'll want to hear."

Wylie pulled himself up to the top of the rock and squinted. "There!" he said, pointing to the largest boulder in sight. "Greely's with her. They were trying to get as high as they could to see if they could spot the *Wayfarer*."

"I don't think we'll be able to see our ship from here," Cosmo said, already clambering over the rocks toward his fellow Alphas. "But that doesn't mean we can't find it!"

The two koalas found Liza at the top of the boulder, scratching shapes onto its surface with a sharp stick. Greely stood a short distance away with his back to the water, staring out at the island.

"I believe the mist over that cluster of trees might indicate a waterfall," Greely called to Liza, who nodded as she continued sketching. "A waterfall means a river, though we cannot determine its course from here."

"Are you trying to map out this island?" Wylie asked curiously.

Liza smiled. "What we can see of it, yes."

"I think we might be able to chart even the parts we can't see." Cosmo stepped forward, and Liza stopped sketching and looked up at him.

"What do you mean, Cosmo?"

The koala Alpha held out the seaweed. "This seaweed was just off the northern coast on a sandy beach until the storm hit. It was caught in the same current as us and swept down to the southern tip of the island."

"That must be the beach the lifeboats were headed for," Liza mused, nodding. "So that's where the *Wayfarer* is, along with the others."

"A sandy beach on the northern side!" Cosmo said eagerly. "And here we are on the pointy southern tip, surrounded by rocks and boulders . . . Does that sound familiar?"

Liza's eyes widened. "The map!"

Greely joined them, frowning down at the sketches on the rock. "So you believe this island is, in fact, the island on the map from the Forgotten Archive?"

Leaning on her staff, Liza gazed out

at the jungle and rocks beyond. "It might just be," she said thoughtfully. "We were on course for it, after all."

"Too bad we don't have the real map," Wylie said with a sigh. "Then we'd know the quickest route."

Liza closed her eyes. "I studied that map extensively," she murmured. "The jungle covers the center—it would take quite some time to make our way through. But there's a path through the caves that leads to the northern beach."

She pointed to the cave entrance, and Cosmo's stomach dropped. "The caves? Underground?"

"That's right." Liza looked at him curiously. "Is that okay, Cosmo?"

"Yes, of course!" Cosmo said a little too brightly. "I was just, um, enjoying the sunshine so much. Seems a shame to go down in the dark."

"But much safer in the event of another storm," Greely pointed out. "That first one developed with surprising speed."

"True, very true," Cosmo agreed. But his heart fluttered anxiously in his chest as the four animals climbed down the boulder and made their way toward the cave entrance.

"Are you sure you're okay?" Wylie whispered once they'd stepped inside the cool, dark cave.

Cosmo nodded and smiled, but he clutched the seaweed tightly for comfort. This was ridiculous, he told himself. He was an Alpha, after all. He'd been in countless situations more frightening: battling with Phantoms, cutting down giant ice spikes on Mt. Shiveer, even preventing the eruption of a volcano! Caves were nothing to fear, Cosmo thought resolutely. Even though they were dark. And cramped. And once he was deep inside, there would be no way to escape quickly if he had to.

Shaking off these thoughts, Cosmo hurried to catch up with Liza. She was stopping every dozen or so steps to scratch arrows into the side of the cave with her staff, each one pointing in the direction from which they'd come. The tunnels were dark and narrow, splitting and forking so many times, Cosmo started to feel dizzy.

"Why are you doing that?" Wylie asked when Liza scratched yet another arrow.

"Just in case we need to retrace our steps," she replied.

"Oh! Great idea."

Greely kept ahead of the others, scouting out forks in the path and identifying which tunnels seemed safest. While Liza and Wylie chatted amiably, Cosmo found he couldn't join in. The deeper into the caves they wandered, the more nervous he felt.

"If this really is the island on the map," Wylie was saying, "that means we might walk right under where that *X* marks the spot—the buried treasure!"

Liza smiled. "You sound like Peck."

"You're not excited about the idea of treasure, Liza?" Wylie asked.

"I'm curious about everything on this island," Liza replied. "Including whatever might be buried in that spot."

"I bet it's—*ouch!*"

Wylie fell to the ground with a thud, and Liza immediately knelt at his side.

"Are you hurt?"

"Nah, I'm okay," Wylie said, blushing a little as he brushed off his knees. "I tripped on that."

He pointed to a thick root partially sticking up from the ground. Cosmo followed its path up the side of the tunnel until it disappeared into the rocky ceiling. His trepidation vanished, and he beamed.

"Goodness, those jungle trees must be massive!" he exclaimed, hurrying over to inspect it more closely. "We're deep underground, and their roots still reach down this far . . ."

Greely stood at the next fork, eyeing the two tunnels. "This one on the left is a dead end," he called to the others. "Let's keep—"

He stopped abruptly, and Liza helped Wylie stand. "What is it, Greely?"

The wolf Alpha's yellow eyes narrowed. "I hear something . . . a rumble, growing louder."

"I don't hear anything . . ." Cosmo trailed off as the root beneath his paw began to tremble. "Oh. *That* rumble."

Before anyone else could speak, dust and dirt sprinkled from overhead. A few pebbles fell with a clatter, immediately followed by a rock roughly the size of Cosmo's head. He dodged it nimbly and looked from Liza to Greely.

"What's happening?"

Greely's expression was grim. "Cave-in."

Suddenly, hundreds of rocks cascaded

down behind him, blocking the tunnel to the right.

"Back the way we came!" cried Liza, but it was already too late. The rumble grew deafening as even more rocks poured into the path behind them, rushing closer in a way that reminded Cosmo of the tidal wave. With no other choice, the four animals raced into the tunnel on the left— the one that dead-ended.

They huddled together in the dark, waiting until the roar of falling rocks gradually trickled to a stop. Cosmo's breathing grew shallow, and his heart was hammering rapidly.

Liza leaned on her staff and studied their surroundings. "Well. We appear to be trapped," she said. Her voice was calm but her eyes flashed with worry.

"Oh no," Cosmo whispered. "We'll never get out. Oh no. Oh no."

Liza looked at him in surprise. "Cosmo, it's not like you to panic! We've been in tighter situations than this before."

"What's going on?" Wylie asked kindly, sitting on the ground next to Cosmo. "You've been acting strange since we entered the caves."

"Well . . ." Cosmo let out a slow breath. "I think I might be a little bit claustrophobic."

Wylie blinked. "What does *claustrophobic* mean?" He peered curiously at Cosmo.

"Afraid of small spaces," Liza explained. "Cosmo, I'm so sorry. I had no idea! Don't worry, Greely and I will get us out of here."

While Wylie tried to calm Cosmo down,

Liza and Greely inspected every inch of the short tunnel.

"I suspect this wasn't always a dead end," Greely said. "These rocks are packed incredibly tight, but there are some cracks."

"Another cave-in, perhaps?" Liza replied.

Greely frowned. "It would seem so. But what caused them?"

"Maybe the question is *who* caused them," Liza mused as she ran her paw over the rocky surface. "Oh, I can feel more roots here. Cosmo's right—those trees really do have an incredible reach."

"That's it!" Wylie jumped up and grabbed Cosmo's arm. "That's how we're going to get out. Cosmo can ask the trees to help us!"

Cosmo blinked. Then a slow smile spread across his face. "Of course!"

He leaped up and hurried to the back of the tunnel, placing both paws on the root that twisted between the dense rocks. His panic subsided as he listened to the tree's advice.

"It's not as thick as it looks," Cosmo murmured at last, and Liza stepped closer.

"The root?"

"No, this wall!" Cosmo kept one paw on the root and reached the other higher until he felt a small rock wiggle. "This one's loose!" He pulled it out and tossed it to the ground. Wylie pried loose the medium-size rock that had been next to it, followed by several more small rocks. Soon, the two koalas had created an opening large enough to see through.

"Greely, you were right!" Cosmo cried. "This tunnel isn't a dead end at all!"

"Nice work, Cosmo," Liza said, looking pleased. "We'll be through these caves and on the beach in no time."

Cosmo grinned, patting the root thankfully. "And I was just starting to like it down here," he joked.

CHAPTER FIVE

"Excellent—that's shaping up to be a fine sail!" Graham beamed at the otters and monkeys busily sewing several of the enormous lily pads together. "Now remember, Eugenie is in charge while I'm gone. Any questions, just ask her!"

Eugenie blushed. "Thanks, Graham. We'll have the sails finished by the time you get back!"

"I have complete faith in you," Graham

said, waving goodbye. He hurried down the beach to join Sir Gilbert and Peck, who were waiting at the edge of the jungle to help him search for the supplies he still needed. "Those lily pads were perfect," he told them excitedly. "I daresay the new *Wayfarer* will be even faster than the old one."

Peck gazed out as several monkeys raised one of the smaller sails. "And they look so much cooler. I love that bright green color!"

"Are you sure the crew can get along without you?" Sir Gilbert asked Graham, who nodded fervently.

"Absolutely. Eugenie is exceptionally clever—she can handle any problems that might arise."

The three Alphas headed into the dense jungle, this time heading east, as they'd already explored the west. "What materials and tools are you still in need of?" Sir Gilbert asked, strolling alongside Graham while Peck hopped ahead, nose buried in the map.

"Nuts, bolts, and washers. And propellers," Graham answered promptly. "Two of them. That's going to be the hardest thing to find, I think."

Sir Gilbert frowned thoughtfully. "If the boat catches wind in its sails to move, why do we need propellers?"

"An excellent question!" Graham replied. "The propellers allow the captain more control over the ship. Sometimes the wind isn't blowing hard enough, or it's not blowing in the direction you want to go. That's when the propellers come in handy." He shook his head. "I should've thought to add them when I first designed the ship. Perhaps we might have avoided crashing."

"This way!" Peck called suddenly, making a sharp left off the path. Sir Gilbert and Graham followed her, brushing vines and low-hanging branches out of the way. The air was thick and sweet from the fragrant pink and yellow flowers blooming on the trees. After a few minutes, the canopy of leaves overhead grew so thick, it completely blocked the sun. The temperature dropped, and the three Alphas trekked through the dark, cool jungle in silence.

Sir Gilbert watched Peck hurry down the path, checking the map every few seconds. "Peck," he called mildly. "Perhaps we should move a bit slower and take the time to observe our surroundings? After all, we don't know where we might find the materials Graham needs."

"Not yet!" Peck replied, quickening her pace. "We're almost there . . ."

"Almost where?" Graham wondered, and Sir Gilbert sighed.

"I suspect Peck is searching for something aside from shipbuilding materials . . ."

The bunny Alpha darted ahead, and her companions lost sight of her. Just as Sir Gilbert was beginning to get concerned, they heard her cry:

"Here! I think I found it!"

Sir Gilbert and Graham followed the sound of her voice, stepping into a small clearing. Peck was in the center, where a patch of dirt stood out inside the grass.

"This is the X, I presume?" Sir Gilbert

asked, his voice a mix of amusement and exasperation. Peck nodded vigorously, double-checking the map.

"Yes—I'm totally positive this is it!" she said. "Help me dig?"

"Peck," Sir Gilbert said slowly. "We really need *supplies*. Not treasure."

"But supplies might be just what we find!" Graham announced before Peck could respond. The two Alphas turned to see him holding up a dirt-encrusted spade. "Found this lying over here in the grass. Apparently, someone *has* buried something!"

"I knew it!" Peck squealed.

"That means someone has been here," Sir Gilbert said. "But who?"

"Only one way to find out!" Graham exclaimed.

They set to work digging, Graham with the spade, Peck and Sir Gilbert with their paws. Peck was wriggling with excitement as she worked.

"What do you think they buried?"

"Hopefully more tools," Graham replied, tossing a pile of dirt over his shoulder. The next time his spade hit the ground, there was a loud *THUNK*. "Aha!" he cried, unearthing the top of a black-and-gold chest.

Peck gasped. "Oh my gosh. We found the buried treasure! Oh, I can't wait to tell Liza!"

But Sir Gilbert wasn't looking at the chest. A smooth, perfectly round stone sticking out of the dirt caught his eye. Unlike the other rocks and pebbles, it was a light purplish blue. He plucked it out and his eyes widened.

"Look at this," Sir Gilbert murmured, showing the others. The perfect imprint of a feather covered one side of the stone, long and graceful—and very familiar. "It looks like . . ."

"A heron feather," Graham finished. He set his spade down and scratched his head. "Do you think Mira left this treasure for us to find?"

Peck clutched the map to her chest, her eyes bright. "I bet we'll know when we see it!"

Eagerly, she reached out and unlatched the clasp on the chest. The lid popped open, and the three Alphas leaned forward.

The chest was filled with grimy gold coins and jewels that were probably colorful beneath their thick coating of dust. For a moment, no one spoke.

"That's it?" Peck said finally, unable to keep the disappointment out of her voice. "The treasure is just . . . well, treasure?"

Sir Gilbert chuckled. "So it would seem."

"But Mira wouldn't lead us to gold and jewels." Peck began digging through the chest's contents. "Maybe there's something else in here . . ."

Graham picked up a coin and squinted at it through his goggles. "Fascinating. This one has a hole in the center."

"Lots of them do," Peck agreed, holding up a handful. "And the ones with no holes have an engraving instead."

"A heron feather?" Sir Gilbert asked, but Peck shook her head.

"An eye."

An uneasy feeling settled over Sir Gilbert as he inspected a coin.

The engraving of a slightly narrowed eye glared up at him beneath all the grime.

"Ah!" Graham cried suddenly. "Bolts!"

"What?" Peck asked.

"Some of these jewels are perfectly shaped to make nuts and bolts. And these coins with the holes would make perfect washers to hold them in place!" Graham plucked a coin with a hole from the chest. "See?" He slid the coin over a glittering sapphire and beamed at Peck. "Looks like this treasure is more valuable than we thought. It just might help us rebuild the *Wayfarer*!"

Peck brightened considerably at this. "Well, in that case, let's get it back to the ship!" She tugged hard at the chest, but the bottom half was still buried, and it wouldn't budge.

"Leave it to me!" Graham picked up his spade and slid it down the back of the chest, deep into the dirt. With a grunt, he pulled down on the top of the spade, and the chest slowly began to tilt. "Almost got it . . ."

Sir Gilbert noticed something slither beneath the dirt like a worm. Or rather, several worms, he thought. In fact, it looked as though the entire ground was moving just underneath the surface.

The trees to their left and right both rustled loudly, and before anyone had time to react . . .

"*Yikes!*"

Graham and the chest soared high into the air, lifted by the palm fronds that had been hidden in the dirt. Two long poles extended from either end of the fronds, connecting the trap to something hidden in the trees. Sir Gilbert gasped in surprise.

"Graham!" Peck cried, staring up at the monkey Alpha. He'd grabbed on to a high tree branch, the chest hanging from his other paw. "Are you okay?"

"Fine and dandy!" Graham replied. "It seems whoever buried this treasure also set a trap—a catapult made of bamboo and palm fronds! Unfortunately for them, the trap backfired."

"What do you mean?" asked Sir Gilbert.

"Because those materials are just what we need for the propellers!" Graham sounded delighted. "If we can get that contraption to the *Wayfarer*, that will be everything I need to rebuild!"

Sir Gilbert smiled. "Outstanding!"

Graham tossed the chest to Sir Gilbert before scrambling down the tree. "Great news, isn't it, Peck?" he asked, clapping her on the shoulder. Peck smiled and nodded, watching her fellow Alphas pull the catapult out from the trees. She pictured the chest filled with grimy coins and shivered despite the heat.

"Peck?" Sir Gilbert said, coming over to stand next to her. "What's wrong?"

"It's my fault Graham walked into that trap," she whispered. "I shouldn't have brought us here. You were right, I was too focused on finding the X on the map, and look what happened!"

"But Graham is perfectly safe now," Sir Gilbert reassured her. "And if you hadn't led us here, we wouldn't have found what we needed to rebuild the *Wayfarer*!"

"That's true," Peck admitted. The two

Alphas glanced back at the chest filled with treasure.

Peck knew Sir Gilbert was wondering the same thing she was: Mira would have never left a trap for them like this one. But someone else had.

The question was, who?

CHAPTER SIX

"Hello, sun! I missed you!"

Cosmo was the first to leave the caves, and he danced a little jig that made Wylie and Liza laugh. Greely followed the others, surveying their new surroundings. The cave behind them cut through a cliff that rose high above their heads. The rocky land that stretched out before them sloped downward. Greely couldn't see what lay beyond, but the smell of salt in the air told him they weren't far from the shore.

"I believe we may have reached the eastern coast of the island," he said. "Or at least, we're very close. If the others made it to the northern beach in their lifeboats, we should be able to reach them soon."

Liza climbed a few nearby rocks, testing their sturdiness with her staff. "Finding a safe path might pose a challenge. Some of these rocks are loose."

Turning, Greely stared up at the cliff. His eyes quickly scanned the crevices and narrow ledges and saw a trail to the top of the cliff—a very steep, dangerous trail, but one that would give him an ideal vantage point.

"I'll climb the cliff," he told the others. "From that height, I will be able to identify a safe path leading to the northern tip."

Cosmo craned his neck to squint at the cliff. "From that height, you just might spot the *Wayfarer!*" he said cheerfully.

"Be careful, Greely," Liza said. "That's a steep climb."

Greely didn't respond—he just leaped nimbly to the first ledge. His instincts kicked in, and his paws quickly found the most stable ridges. The sound of the others' voices was soon lost to the wind, and Greely welcomed the silence.

It wasn't long before he stood at the edge of the cliff, gazing out at the island. The sea sparkled to his left, and the beach appeared to be covered in pebbles. To his right, the jungle trees were so thick Greely couldn't see the ground, although he did spot a small tar pit nestled among the trees. The terrain between the cliff and the beach was a maze of rocks, but Greely spotted a path almost immediately. Unfortunately, it led south. A shame, he thought, because it was almost a straight line, as if someone—or something—had carved their way through.

Just as Greely thought this, an odd smell reached his nostrils; a rotten, sickly sweet smell. Crouching low, he prowled along the edge of the cliff until he spotted a fork in the path. One branch led to the beach, where the water had a strange green tinge to it. The color gradually grew darker and darker, leading out to the source: a ship.

But it wasn't the *Wayfarer*.

Greely cataloged every detail as quickly as possible. The ship was black and purple, with dirty patched-up sails and a seemingly perpetual cloud of smog surrounding it. The green sludge in the water clearly came from the ship; even from this distance, Greely could see barrels of the nasty stuff on the deck, all emitting the same unnaturally green glow. His gaze moved to the figurehead on the bow, which at first glance appeared to be a black fish . . . until Greely spotted the single glaring eye on its head.

The ship was moving slowly up the coast, spreading sludge through the water. As it turned slightly, Greely caught sight of a black flag bearing its name: *Befouler*.

Memories of the storm flashed through Greely's mind: the gray smog swirled with purple, that same green hue to the water. The storm had hit so quickly, and now Greely knew why: It had not been a natural storm.

It was caused by Phantoms.

Greely continued along the edge of the cliff, and a bay came into view. One look at the strange ramshackle structures covering the bay, and Greely knew this was where the *Befouler* was headed.

Without wasting another second, Greely made his way down the cliff at top speed, leaping from ledge to ledge with extraordinary precision. When he reached the bottom, Liza took one look at his expression and immediately grew somber.

"What's wrong, Greely?"

The wolf Alpha filled the others in quickly. "I believe they created the storm that caused us to shipwreck here."

"That might explain the cave-in, too," Cosmo said, shaking his head. "Destruction is what the Phantoms do best."

"Not just Phantoms," Wylie whispered with a shiver. *"Pirate* Phantoms."

Liza nodded grimly. "Pirate Phantoms who just might know we're here."

Wylie swallowed. "The other Alphas, and the crew . . . You don't think the Phantoms got them, do you?"

"There was no sign of any animal on that ship," Greely said immediately. "However . . ."

"The *Befouler* is sure to reach the northern beach, and the others, before we do," Liza finished. She looked from Greely to Cosmo, and knew they were thinking the same thing.

"What?" Wylie looked at each of them in turn. "What's going on?"

Cosmo smiled grimly. "It looks like we need to change our plans."

CHAPTER SEVEN

Just off the northern shore of the island, several animals crowded behind the overturned *Wayfarer*. Each one was holding on to one of the thick vines tied to the mast and the deck's railing, waiting excitedly for Graham's command.

"On three!" the monkey Alpha called through a conch shell he was using as a megaphone. "One . . . two . . . three! *Heave!*"

With grunts and shouts, the crew pulled

as hard as they could. Slowly, the *Wayfarer* began to tilt toward them, until finally it landed in the water with a splash.

"Well done!" Graham cried, beaming at the sight of the lily pad sails blowing in the wind, and the crew cheered. "Now we can get to work installing the propellers and repairing the hole in the hull. Everyone, please see Eugenie for your assignments!"

The crew huddled around Eugenie, who began dividing them into groups: one to clean the mounds of grimy jewels and coins from the treasure chest; the second to separate them into piles of makeshift nuts, bolts, and washers; and a third to drag the two giant propellers onto the ship. As the animals got to work, Graham spotted Sir Gilbert and Peck on a large dune just up the beach. Sir Gilbert was peering through a spyglass, while Peck was, as usual, studying the map. She had been a bit despondent ever since the incident with the treasure chest and the trap, and Graham decided to go cheer her up.

"Good news, my friends!" he called as he hiked up the steep dune. "Now that the *Wayfarer* is right side up again, the rest of the repairs should go quickly!"

"Awesome!" said Peck, but her smile wasn't as enthusiastic as usual. "I'm really glad all those coins and stuff were useful."

"*Quite* useful," Graham agreed. "And those propellers as well. We never would have found what we needed if you hadn't gone off course to look for treasure!"

He said it kindly, but Peck still looked glum. Graham scratched his head, trying to think of another way to cheer her up.

But before he could say anything else, Sir Gilbert cleared his throat and lowered the spyglass.

"I believe we might have a problem," he said, handing the spyglass to Graham. "Can you look over there and tell me what you see?"

Graham held the spyglass to his eye and aimed it in the direction Sir Gilbert was pointing. Movement caught his eye, and he frowned, adjusting the focus and zooming in on three figures making their way through the rocks many miles away. Two of the figures were dark and rather blobby, each with a single unblinking eye. The other was a familiar koala.

"Phantoms," Graham said in disbelief. "And it looks like they have Wylie!"

Peck jumped up in alarm, her map

forgotten. "What? Are you sure?"

"One's wearing a green tricorne hat," Graham reported, twisting the viewfinder. "The other has what appears to be a purple bandanna around his head, and . . . and a staff. Oh no." Lowering the spyglass, he stared at Sir Gilbert. "That looks like Liza's staff!"

"My thoughts precisely," Sir Gilbert replied grimly. "It appears that there are pirate Phantoms on this island, and I'm afraid they may have captured our missing companions."

Peck shook her head. "There's no way any Phantoms are clever enough to outsmart Liza, Greely, and Cosmo. Can I see that spyglass?"

Graham handed it over, and Peck quickly found the two black shapes. When she lowered the spyglass, to Graham's amazement, she was smiling a real Peck smile—excited and a little bit mischievous.

"Take another look," she said, handing the spyglass back to Graham. "Don't those Phantoms look a little bit . . . *strange*?"

Graham peered through the spyglass again. "They are rather odd-looking. Shiny and sticky, like . . ." A smile spread across his face. "Rather like two animals covered in tar."

"Exactly," Peck said with a grin. "I don't know what they're up to, but I'm going to help. First, I'm going to need some mud."

Back on the eastern side of the island, Greely lurked behind a tree and watched the trail into the jungle impatiently.

He had raced ahead of the others to spy on the *Befouler*, which was now moored in the bay. Greely's fur was still soaked from the hour he'd spent lurking behind a rock in the shallow, murky water. But that was a small price to pay for the information he'd learned spying on the two pirate Phantoms standing guard on the dock— mostly information about the *Befouler*'s nefarious captain.

At last, he heard Cosmo's voice and the sound of footsteps. Greely stepped out of his hiding place, and for a split second, he was rendered speechless.

Wylie was flanked by two Phantoms. Or rather, two Phantom-like creatures.

"What do you think?" one asked Greely.

"Impressive," Greely admitted. "I had my doubts about your idea, but you two really do look the part."

While Greely had been in the bay, the others had made a quick trip to the tar pit he'd spotted in the jungle. Wylie had helped Liza and Cosmo coat themselves in tar from head to toe, complete with tar-covered vines as tentacles. Then, he'd found two round white shells, drawn a black pupil with charcoal on the center of each, and affixed them to the middle of Liza's and Cosmo's faces. Cosmo had squashed and twisted his pointy hat into a tricorne shape, and Liza wore Greely's purple cloak as a bandanna.

"*Arrr,*" Cosmo growled. "Me thinks you've mistaken us for some landlubbers, matey!"

Liza chuckled. "So, Greely. Any information for us before we board the *Befouler*?"

"The ship belongs to Captain Red Eye," Greely reported. "I didn't see him, but I overheard two Phantoms talking about him on the dock. They believe his eye has some sort of special ability, though there seemed to be some debate over what that ability is. One said Red Eye can spot traitors, while the other said his eye can read minds."

Liza's eyebrows rose skeptically. "Hmm. Anything else?"

"The dock where the *Befouler* is moored is only temporary," Greely said. "Whatever business the Phantoms have on this island, they don't plan on staying long."

"Well, whaddaya say, matey?" Liza asked him with a grin. "Shall we board the *Befouler* and uncover Captain Red Eye's dastardly plot?"

"Aye, aye!" Cosmo cried, and the two Alphas waved goodbye to Greely and Wylie before setting off down the path to the bay. When the shore came into view, Cosmo gasped.

"Ew."

The bay had probably been beautiful before the Phantoms arrived, with white sand and turquoise waters like the rest of the coast. But now, a complicated series of docks connected by walkways and ladders covered the area, all built from what looked like dark, rotting wood. Slimy moss and dried seaweed hung from the ramshackle structure, which completely surrounded the *Befouler*. Two Phantoms stood watch on the walkway overlooking the sea, and when Cosmo squinted, he saw gears and pulleys.

"Is that a gate?" he asked Liza in a low voice.

The panda Alpha nodded. "To let the ship in and out," she whispered back.

Graham could have built a much better contraption, Cosmo thought with a pang of sadness. And without all this filth and mess, too.

Straightening his smashed tricorne hat more firmly on his tar-covered head, Cosmo followed Liza up the nearest steps. The wind carried sounds of cackling laughter and loud chatter from the *Befouler*.

"Now, remember the story we came up with," Liza reminded Cosmo as they crossed the first walkway. "Our pirate ship had a mutiny, and we're looking for another crew to join."

"Got it." Cosmo began climbing the

ladder to the next platform, Liza right behind him. "And we heard Captain Red Eye is the best—no, the *worst* pirate captain ever to sail the high seas! The foulest, vilest, most wicked of all the pirate Phantoms . . . They'll think that's a compliment, right?"

"Absolutely."

Cosmo reached the platform and helped Liza up the last few rungs. "Captain Red Eye, the rudest, most revolting and fright—Ew, scuzzy!"

Wrinkling his nose, Cosmo hopped out of the puddle he'd accidentally stepped in. Whatever it contained managed to be both slimy and fuzzy. Cosmo tried in vain to wipe the stuff from his feet, but it clung to the tar like glue.

"Scuzzy? That really be you?"

Liza and Cosmo whirled around to see a Phantom emerge from the shadows of a nearby platform. He wore a red bandanna around his head, and an eye patch made from what appeared to be a black, shriveled palm frond covered his single eye.

The Phantom moved forward, tripping over his tentacles a little bit. "Scuzzy?" he said again, sounding eager. "It's me, Luglow!"

"Aye, Luglow!" Liza said, making her voice low and gruff. "It be me, Scuzzy!"

Beaming, Luglow threw his tentacles around Cosmo in an embrace. "My old pal Scuzzy! I can't believe it!"

"Here, Luglow!" Liza said, tapping the Phantom's back with one of her vines. "That's me fr—Um, me fellow pirate, um . . . Scummy!"

Cosmo stifled a giggle as Luglow pulled away. "Ah, my mistake! Well, Scummy, any pal of Scuzzy's is a pal of mine!"

Luglow turned to Liza—or rather, he turned to the ladder, and Liza quickly sidestepped in front of it so that she and the Phantom were eye-to-eye patch. "So, Scuzzy, what brings you here?"

Keeping her gruff pirate voice, Liza launched into the story she and Cosmo had cooked up. "And we've heard tales about Captain Red Eye," she finished. "How fierce and fearsome he is, and—"

"And foul!" Cosmo added, and Luglow nodded vehemently. "And vile!"

"And we were hoping we might join the crew of the *Befouler*," Liza finished. "Can you help us out, Luglow? For . . . for old times' sake?"

Luglow sniffled and wiped a tear from the corner of his eye patch. "What a terrible tale, Scuzzy," he blubbered. "Of course I'll help you!"

Liza and Cosmo shared a grin. "*Arr!*" Cosmo cried triumphantly.

"*Arrrrr!*" yelled Luglow, tentacles flailing. "Come on, the captain is hosting a feast on board tonight. I was running late—my eye patch fell off in the jungle, and I got lost searching for it—but I'm glad that happened because I might not've run into you otherwise! Follow me, mateys!"

With that, the Phantom spun around and walked right off the walkway. A loud splash followed, and Liza and Cosmo hurried to the edge.

"Luglow!" Liza called. "Are you okay?"

There was a gurgling sound, and then: "Aye!"

The Alphas stepped back as Luglow pulled himself up the ladder. "Got a little turned around there!" he said, flapping his tentacles and spraying them with water. "Right, then—which way is the ship?"

"This way." Liza grabbed Luglow and spun him around so he was facing the *Befouler*. The Phantom barreled down the platform, Liza and Cosmo right behind him, and stopped only when he bumped into another ladder. "*Arr!*" he said loudly, grabbing the rungs. "Some scallywag must've moved this again."

Liza and Cosmo followed Luglow up the ladder. They stayed on either side of the Phantom as he led them down the next walkway, nudging him when he veered off course. At last, the trio reached the plank leading up to the *Befouler*.

"Here we go, Scuzzy," Cosmo said, casting Liza a nervous but excited glance. She smiled encouragingly.

"Here we go, Scummy."

Luglow wobbled up the plank. Adjusting his shell eye, Cosmo followed, with Liza bringing up the rear. The sounds of laughter and clanging dishes coming from the captain's cabin were louder now, and it sounded as though the crew were chanting. When they stepped onto the deck, Cosmo realized it was a sea shanty, a type of song pirates sang while sailing the seas.

"He's the foulest pirate on the seas of high!
Red Eye! Red Eye!

He's clever, he's spry, his gaze is sly!
Red Eye! Red Eye!
When you see him coming, your end is nigh!
Red Eye! Red Eye!"

Luglow sighed happily. "Isn't that a great song, Scuzzy?" he asked, leading them toward the captain's cabin. "I heard other Phantoms hate music, can you imagine? Not us pirate Phantoms, though. Gotta keep yerself entertained when you're not plunderin' and piratin'!"

"*Arr,*" Liza agreed, watching as Luglow felt around the wooden door with his tentacles until he found the rusty latch. He pushed the door open, and the chanting and laughter stopped abruptly.

"Captain Red Eye!" Luglow announced, stepping inside. "I've found us two new crew members—my old pal Scuzzy, and his old pal Scummy!"

Liza and Cosmo entered the cabin. A long wooden table took up most of the room, with equally long benches on either side and a large black chair at the head, which was in shadows. Plates piled high with dried seaweed and bowls of brown muck covered the table, along with mugs filled with what looked like swamp water. Smog drifted in through the open window, thick and greenish gray.

The Phantoms seated on the benches turned toward the door, squinting at Liza and Cosmo with obvious suspicion. At the head of the table, a dark figure leaned forward, and an enormous bloodshot eye appeared. For the first time in her life, Liza was grateful for smog. Their disguises suddenly felt flimsy, and she hoped the thick, filthy air would help conceal their identities.

"Is that so, Luglow?" Captain Red Eye stood slowly, his voice a low rumble. "And what makes you think I'd be willing to take two strangers on as crew?"

"I can vouch for Scuzzy, sir," Luglow said, and Cosmo noticed he sounded nervous now. "We sailed together on the same crew once, long ago!"

Cosmo shivered under that fierce red gaze. He thought of the rumor that Captain Red Eye could read minds, and he thought *I am Scummy, pirate Phantom!* as hard as he could.

Liza stepped forward, her staff thumping on the wooden floor. "It's true, Captain," she said in a growly voice.

"Luglow and I go way back."

A beam of sunlight shone through the window, landing on Liza as she spoke. A sparkle on the top of her staff caught Cosmo's eye, and he froze.

Captain Red Eye noticed it, too. "So, Luglow," he said with a sneer. "Can you explain to us why, exactly, your old pal Scuzzy is carrying a staff topped with what is unmistakably an Alpha Stone?"

Cosmo twitched nervously, but Liza remained calm. "Aye, this be an Alpha Stone," she said gruffly, slamming her staff on the floor for emphasis. "I stole it from the panda Alpha after Scummy and I trapped them in a pit right here on this island!"

Murmurs and whispers broke out among the Phantoms, and Captain Red Eye roared:

"Silence!" He waited several seconds, and when no one dared to make so much as a peep, he squinted at Liza. "Did you, now? *All* of the Alphas?"

It was a risk, but Liza decided to take it. "Aye, sir," she said. "You don't have to worry about those Alphas interfering with your plans, whatever they may be!"

Captain Red Eye leaned back in his chair, considering this. "That's quite an achievement," he said at last. "Perhaps you'd like to regale my crew with the tale of how you managed such a fantastic feat?"

Liza took a deep breath. She couldn't tell whether the captain actually believed her or not. But before she could speak, someone behind them piped up.

"If it's a tale ye be lookin' for, I've got one for ye!"

Everyone turned to stare at the newcomer, including Captain Red Eye. There in the doorway stood the strangest Phantom that Liza had ever seen: dark brown, lumpy, and tentacle-less, with two hooks for arms and two thick peg legs. But the Phantom's voice was familiar, though Liza could tell she was trying to disguise it.

Oh, Peck, Liza thought in alarm. *What are you doing here?*

CHAPTER EIGHT

Every eye in the captain's cabin was on
Peck, including the reddest, wateriest
eye she'd ever seen. With as much flair
as possible, Peck stomped into the smog-
filled cabin on the peg legs Sir Gilbert had
fashioned out of branches. The two hooks
were courtesy of Graham; he'd made her
swear to take care of them, as they were
used to attach the mainsail to the boom
on the *Wayfarer*. The rest of her costume

was smelly, dark mud and a blob of thick sea foam that Eugenie had formed into a Phantom eye with a black rock pupil. Peck avoided looking at Liza and Cosmo, but she felt sure they recognized her. The Phantoms around the table were squinting through the smog, and Peck took care not to get too much closer.

"So, it's a story ye be wantin'?" Peck growled, turning so her sea-foam blob met the captain's bloodshot eye. "I guarantee the best tale ye ever heard . . . but first, I demand to know what ye be doin' on *my* island."

Captain Red Eye snarled, shoving aside his plate with his tentacle. "*Your* island? I never heard of no other pirate Phantom on this here island!"

"You never heard of Bandanna Anna?"

"Who?"

"Bandanna Anna!" Peck repeated, glaring around at the crew. "That's Bandy to you lot."

"And what right do ye have callin' this *your* island, Bandanna Anna?" Captain Red Eye said in a dangerously low voice.

"I washed up on these shores ages ago." Peck paused for dramatic effect. "Right after I lost my last feeler."

She waved her right hook for emphasis, and several Phantoms winced and curled their tentacles.

"How'd you lose your feelers?" Luglow asked in a shaking voice, still facing the door.

"Quiet, Luglow!" Captain Red Eye barked. "I'll be askin' the questions. Now," he said, facing Peck. "How'd you lose your feelers?"

Peck smiled beneath her mud mask. "Well, that be the tale, don't it? All I need before I be tellin' it is to know what business the *Befouler* has here. What say ye?"

The Phantom crew turned to Captain Red Eye, but he remained silent.

"I do love a good tale!" one said.

"C'mon, Captain! We can trust a fellow pirate, can't we?" called another.

Captain Red Eye's gaze never wavered from Peck. Then, a sneer curled his lips.

"Aye, very well," he said, leaning back in his chair. "But be warned, Bandanna Anna. If this tale ain't the best, the greatest, the *foulest* tale we ever heard, you're comin' out to sea with us—and walkin' the plank."

The Phantoms all chuckled darkly at this, and Peck swallowed nervously.

"Aye, it will be," she promised.

"We'll see." Captain Red Eye lifted

his mug and took a sip of greenish gunk. "Now then, business first. You ever heard of the Alphas?"

The crew hissed and sneered, and it took all of Peck's willpower not to glance at Liza or Cosmo. "*Arrr*, those . . . those scallywags!"

"*Arrrr!*" several Phantoms growled in agreement, and the captain smirked.

"These two"—he gestured to Cosmo and Liza—"claim to have caught the Alphas in a trap . . . a claim which I have yet to verify," he added menacingly. "And believe me, I will. You see, I too set a trap for the Alphas, just in case they started snoopin' around where they shouldn't."

"The buried treasure!" Peck blurted out, then slapped a hook over her tar-covered mouth.

Captain Red Eye growled. "And just what do ye know about our treasure, missy?"

"Nothing!" Peck said, recovering quickly. "We pirates always have treasure to bury, aye?"

"Aye, we did!" Luglow cried. "And we set such a clever trap, you shoulda seen it. Noisy work, though. I think we might've caused a little earthquake or something 'cause the ground beneath us started to rumble and—"

"Enough, Luglow!" Captain Red Eye bellowed, and Luglow fell silent. "You see," the captain continued, leering at Peck through the smog. "We needed to keep our treasure safe, and this here island was the perfect place. Now we're ready to take the next step in my plan."

Peck matched his leer. "And what plan be that?"

"The *Befouler* has been bestowed with great powers of pollution," Captain Red Eye told her. "We've been using this here island to test it out, sailing close to the coasts. When it's in motion, this ship can poison the waters, bring about storms, open Phantom portals . . . even cause tidal waves." The captain stood slowly, placing two tentacles on the table and leaning forward. "Imagine our dismay when one of those tidal waves wrecked the *Wayfarer*!"

Another wave of laughter rumbled around the table. "A happy coincidence for us that the Alphas also happened upon this island where we chose to bury our treasure," Captain Red Eye finished. "All we had to do was set a trap to protect it from their greedy paws. Now they're shipwrecked, and the *Befouler* is ready to set sail for the coasts of Jamaa. We'll destroy the land from the water, and the Alphas won't be there to get in our way!"

Cheers erupted at this statement, and Peck stood there in shock. Then Liza yelled, "*Arr!* Destroy Jamaa!" and, after a moment of staring at her in surprise, Peck and Cosmo caught on.

"Down with the Alphas!"

"*Arrr!*"

"And now, Bandanna Anna," Captain Red Eye said once the ruckus had died down. "I believe you've promised us a tale the likes of which we've never heard. Or else . . ."

Luglow giggled. "Or else she'll be walkin' the plank!"

Peck could feel Liza and Cosmo staring

at her, and she knew they must be worried. But when she'd been putting together her disguise, in the back of her head she'd started concocting a story about her hooks and peg legs. Peck *loved* stories, and she knew she could spin a great one.

Turning to Cosmo, she whispered: "Open the door. The smoggier, the better."

Then she faced the table and smiled. "A tale the likes of which ye've never heard? Aye, I think I can manage that."

And with that, Peck leaped up onto the table, kicking aside a bowl of muck, and began to sing.

"It was a dark and stormy night
When my first feeler I did lose.
A chest, with coins that shone so bright,
So wrongly I did choose.

I took that chest so heavy with gold.
The lid snapped down like a mitt.
It plunged into the sea so cold
And took my feeler with it!"

As Peck sang, she stomped her peg legs on the table in rhythm, and several of the Phantoms began clapping their tentacles along with her as she launched into the chorus. No one noticed when Cosmo opened the door, and more swirling, greenish-gray smog drifted into the cabin.

"Yo ho! Yo ho! My name be Bandy.
Yo ho! Yo ho! My feelers were lost at sea!"

To her right, Peck saw Cosmo trying to hide his giggles. She grinned and added a little dance before continuing.

> *"Now the second time I came upon*
> *A chest with yet more treasure,*
> *The lesson I'd learned, it was long gone,*
> *For gold gives me so much pleasure.*
>
> *This chest was heavy, it weighed a ton.*
> *In truth, it needed a diet.*
> *For lurking inside wasn't gold I'd won*
> *But a sea beast with a taste for pirate!"*

The Phantoms roared with laughter and waved their mugs in unison. This time, they joined in on the chorus.

> *"Yo ho! Yo ho! Her name be Bandy.*
> *Yo ho! Yo ho! Her feelers were lost at sea!"*

Peck spun around in the center of the table, enjoying herself so much she almost forgot she was on a Phantom pirate ship in the smog-filled cabin of a dangerous captain. She danced and stomped in time with the crew's clanking mugs, then continued.

"Well, the next loss I suffered was quite a shock,
I don't mind tellin' ye.
This tale involves a rickety dock
That cost me my feeler three!"

As Peck prepared to finish the verse, she stomped on the edge of a plate. It launched a mound of seaweed across the table—right into Captain Red Eye's red eye.

A terrified hush fell over the cabin.

Peck froze, one peg leg sticking straight out in front of her, as the Phantom crew lowered their mugs. Everyone stared in horror at the captain as he slowly wiped the seaweed off. His eye was more bloodshot than ever, and it glared right at Peck.

"Well, Bandanna Anna," Captain Red Eye hissed. "It seems your story wasn't worthy of *ahh . . . ahhhh . . . CHOO!*"

The force of his powerful sneeze almost knocked Peck off her peg legs. She gazed at his watering eye and was hit with a realization.

"Oh, *that's* why your eye's so red!" Peck exclaimed, forgetting to use her pirate voice. "You're allergic to seaweed!"

Behind her, Luglow giggled. "A pirate allergic to seaweed! Now *that's* a good story!"

The rest of the crew was so shocked,

they didn't even notice Peck's voice had changed. They just stared at Captain Red Eye, who was now attempting to hide the fact that he had the sniffles.

"It's true!" one said. "It's the seaweed that did it!"

"His eye doesn't have special powers!" another cackled. "Just allergies!"

The Phantoms began to jeer and laugh as Captain Red Eye sneezed again.

"You ever heard such a funny story, Scuzzy?" Luglow howled, slapping Liza on the back. And to Peck's horror, the white shell that had been Liza's Phantom eye flew off.

Cosmo and Peck gasped. Not even the smog could hide Liza's face. Silence fell once more as the crew gaped at her.

The captain glared with his hazy eye,

and now his lips curled up in a wicked smile. Triumphantly, he pointed a tentacle at Liza, Cosmo, and Peck, and bellowed:

"Alphas! Get them!"

Without a word, the three Alphas fled the *Befouler*, the Phantom crew hot on their heels.

CHAPTER NINE

After watching Liza and Cosmo board the *Befouler*, Greely had searched the nearby jungle for vines. He returned with a bundle of them between his teeth to find Wylie right where he'd left him, lying flat on his belly on top of the highest platform.

Greely dropped the vines. "No signs of trouble so far?"

Wylie bit his lip. "Not exactly . . . but a few minutes ago, another Phantom showed up. A really odd Phantom."

"Odd?"

"He didn't have any tentacles," Wylie said. "Just two hooks, and two peg legs! And he was still pretty short."

"Hmm." Greely stared at the *Befouler*, thinking. Then realization dawned, and he almost smiled. "Ah. Peck."

"Where?" Wylie asked, glancing around eagerly.

"I believe that Phantom was, in fact, Peck in disguise," Greely said. "When I was collecting these vines, I saw what looked remarkably like bunny prints in the dirt, leading up to a mud puddle."

"Oh!" Wylie beamed. "That means the others are close, doesn't it?"

"Quite close," came a voice behind them. Greely turned around sharply.

"Sir Gilbert!" he exclaimed, then cleared his throat. "I trust you've enjoyed your stay on the island?"

The tiger Alpha chuckled. "It's been quite the adventure: quicksand, buried treasure—"

"You found the treasure?" Wylie interrupted, eyes shining. "Was it gold?"

"Sadly, yes. Jewels as well."

"How dull," said Greely dryly.

"Indeed," Sir Gilbert agreed. "Fortunately, Graham has made good use of them."

He glanced at the *Befouler* and frowned thoughtfully. "Liza and Cosmo are also on board, I presume?"

Greely nodded. "Though in disguises less creative than Peck's, it would seem."

"We were going to rig a trap for the Phantoms," Wylie told Sir Gilbert excitedly.

"Just in case things go wrong."

Sir Gilbert nodded, glancing at the pile of vines. "A net?"

"That was my initial idea," Greely said. "But we wouldn't be able to build one fast enough. However . . ." He walked to the edge of the platform and pointed to an enormous brown lily pad floating in the bay.

"Ah," Sir Gilbert said. "Allow me to help."

While Wylie watched the *Befouler*, the two Alphas quickly tied the vines end to end to form a long rope. Then Greely hopped down to the walkway below their platform, leaped to the lowest walkway, and slipped into the shallow bay. He swam silently over to the lily pad, then called up to Sir Gilbert:

"Now!"

Sir Gilbert tossed the rope down, and

Greely caught it with his teeth. He cut a small hole on the edge of the thick lily pad with his claw, then looped the rope through and tied a tight knot. He could hear thumping and chanting coming from the *Befouler*, as if the crew was singing a sea shanty.

After double-checking to make sure the knot was secure, Greely leaped back up to the walkway and hurried to rejoin the others on the highest platform. Sir Gilbert handed him a section of the rope, and together they began to heave the enormous lily pad, heavy and dripping with mud and slime, up to their platform.

"I must confess," Sir Gilbert said as they worked. "I was a bit angry with you for cutting the ropes to our lifeboat before everyone had boarded. It seemed a rash decision, especially for you."

Greely arched a brow. "It was strategic. A tidal wave was coming, and I knew we didn't have time to get everyone on the lifeboat."

"We might have, had you allowed us to help free Wylie's leg," Sir Gilbert countered. "And even if we hadn't, we would have stayed together."

"But nowhere near the *Wayfarer* and the rest of the crew," Greely said. "Graham was on your lifeboat—I assume he's been successful at rebuilding the ship?"

"Quite successful, yes. Ah, I see." Sir Gilbert paused for a moment. "You made the right decision. I should have seen that."

Greely kept his eyes on the lily pad, but after a moment, he dipped his head in acknowledgment of the compliment. He had always found himself more at odds with Sir Gilbert than the other Alphas. But after facing so many dangers together, they'd grown to respect each other . . . if a bit reluctantly.

With a final heave, the two Alphas pulled the lily pad onto the platform. In the silence that followed, Greely's ears flicked.

"Something's wrong."

"They stopped singing," Wylie whispered from his spot at the edge of the platform. Greely and Sir Gilbert stood still, listening. Then:

"*Alphas! Get them!*"

"They're coming." Greely grabbed the edge of the lily pad and carried it to the end of the platform. Sir Gilbert did the same with the other end, while Wylie scurried to hide behind him. He peered out from behind the tiger Alpha's cloak when the doors to the captain's cabin burst open.

Liza and Cosmo sprinted out onto the deck first, and Wylie immediately noticed that Liza's shell eye was gone. They were followed by a Phantom with hooks who was hopping remarkably fast considering she had peg legs—Peck, Wylie remembered with a grin.

His happiness soon turned to fear when at least a dozen real Phantoms charged out of the cabin, chasing the animals down the walkway. A Phantom wearing an eye patch tripped and fell onto a lower platform.

"Help!" he yelped, rolling around on the wooden planks, his tentacles flailing.

"Don't let the sea beast get my feelers!"

Captain Red Eye emerged from the cabin last, his bloodshot eye wide and wet as he watched the chase. Greely stiffened, watching the captain's gaze travel up and up until it landed on the two Alphas on the highest platform.

"It's a trap!" the captain roared, but it was too late. His crew slowed and stared around in confusion right below Greely and Sir Gilbert, who let go of the lily pad at the same time. It landed on the crew like a giant soggy blanket, muffling their yelps and pinning them to the walkway.

"Run!" Sir Gilbert grabbed Wylie and leaped down the series of platforms, Greely right behind him. They joined the other Alphas, but there was no time for a happy reunion. The animals ran as fast as they could into the jungle, and it was several minutes before Captain Red Eye's shouts and threats finally faded.

CHAPTER TEN

Graham was the first to spot his fellow Alphas when they emerged from the jungle. He ran down the beach to greet them, Eugenie on his heels.

"Are the Phantoms coming?" Graham called the second the others were in earshot.

"They didn't follow." Liza leaned on her staff and tried to catch her breath. "Did they, Greely?"

Greely eyed the jungle for a long

126

moment, then nodded. "Our trap gave us the time we needed to escape. And they will likely be more concerned with setting sail for Jamaa than finding us."

"The Phantoms are sailing for Jamaa?" Eugenie gasped. "How awful!"

"Yes, we must—oh my goodness!" Liza gazed at the ship out in the water. "Is that really the *Wayfarer*?"

Graham beamed with pride. "It is!" he said. "Although she's like a new ship in so many ways, I was thinking perhaps we should rename her."

Eugenie squirmed excitedly. "Great idea! Anyone have any suggestions?"

The six Alphas, Eugenie, and Wylie fell silent, marveling at the ship. In place of white sails, the masts were now holding thick, bright green lily pads stitched with fine leaves of a much darker green. Purple and blue shells covered the hole in the hull, and the entire ship sparkled thanks to the multicolored jewels and gold coins Graham had used as nuts and bolts. Best of all, though they could only see it when they took turns using the spyglass, was the bow, where Graham had embedded the stone with the heron-feather imprint.

The overall effect was so beautiful, Peck found her eyes filling with tears.

"I've got it," she said at last. "The *Spirit of Jamaa*."

Sir Gilbert bowed his head. "It's just perfect, Peck."

"Indeed." Liza wiped her eyes and cleared her throat. "And speaking of Jamaa, we need to move fast if we're going to intercept the *Befouler*!"

A few hours later, the *Spirit of Jamaa* glided effortlessly across the water. The Alphas stood at their stations once more, watching as the island disappeared behind them. As fascinating as the new land had been, they were happy to be making their way home—and eager to defend it.

Liza stood at the helm, gripping the wheel and marveling at the speed of the ship.

"It's faster than ever!" she called to Graham, who gave her two thumbs-up before disappearing belowdecks to check on the propellers.

"Thanks to the Phantoms' treasure," Cosmo said with a giggle. "It's funny, isn't it, Peck? You thought gold and jewels would be boring, but they turned out to be just what we needed!"

Peck blushed. "They did, yeah." She cast a sheepish look at Sir Gilbert. "I guess it's a good thing I was so obsessed, huh?"

Sir Gilbert chuckled. "If you hadn't found that treasure, we wouldn't have a working ship. *Obsessed* might be too harsh a term, but I think your enthusiasm paid off."

"I bet Captain Red Eye isn't going to be too happy about your thievery, *Bandanna Anna*," Cosmo added, and Peck laughed.

"Probably not!"

A gruff shout from the crow's nest caused them to fall silent. "We're coming up on the *Befouler*!" Greely pointed, and everyone stared at the horizon. The sky above the ship was dark, and the waters were churning.

"Captain Red Eye seems to be preparing another storm in the hopes of destroying our ship once again," Sir Gilbert said grimly.

Liza lifted her chin. "That's not going to happen. The *Spirit of Jamaa* can take whatever those pirate Phantoms throw at us. Everyone, to your stations!"

The crew leaped into action. Liza spun the wheel as hard as she could to the left, calling instructions to the crew, who adjusted the pulleys and manned the sails. Belowdecks, Graham and Eugenie tinkered with the propellers, and soon the *Spirit* was sailing even faster than before. In the crow's nest, Greely braced himself against the wind and watched the *Befouler* grow larger, along with the trail of green slime it left it its wake.

"We're gaining on them!" he called down to the others. "Ready the rope!"

Sir Gilbert joined Cosmo, Peck, and Wylie in tying an extra-long rope made from dozens of vines to the ship's sturdiest mast, ensuring the knot was as tight as possible. The *Befouler* was so close now, they could see Captain Red Eye's snarl from where he stood behind the helm.

"My treasure!" he howled when he saw the *Spirit*'s shining nuts and bolts. "My jewels, my gold! You'll pay for that, Alphas!"

Captain Red Eye began shouting orders to his crew, and Liza grimaced.

"Brace yourselves!" she cried, and a moment later:

BOOM!

Brown and black goop shot from the *Befouler*'s cannons, spattering all over the sides and deck of the Spirit. Liza wrenched the wheel hard, and now the ships were side by side.

BOOM!

More gunk rained down on the *Spirit*, causing the crew to duck. Liza steered the ship directly into a cresting wave, which washed over the deck and rinsed the slimy goop away. The jewels and coins sparkled more brightly than ever, and Captain Red Eye scowled.

"You'll have to do better than that!" Cosmo taunted, dancing a little jig and waving at the crew of the *Befouler*. The distraction worked: Captain Red Eye roared and ordered another round of goop fired, and the Phantoms scurried to obey.

BOOM! BOOM! BOOM!

This time, the *Spirit*'s crew was ready. As the gobs of muck flew toward them, they pulled out the extra-strong strips of bark Graham had given them right before they'd set sail. Each monkey, panda, fox, and otter picked a gob, swung back, and . . .

Thwack!

They hit the gobs, sending them flying back over to the *Befouler* and causing the Phantoms to scatter.

In the chaos of the battle, none of the Phantoms saw Peck jump from the bow of the *Spirit* to the bow of the *Befouler*, the end of the vine rope in her paw.

She worked at lightning speed, triple-tying the rope in a knot around the *Befouler*'s bow, then leaping back to the *Spirit* just as another *BOOM!* sounded.

Peck landed on the deck next to Cosmo, along with several spatters of goop, and gave Liza the thumbs-up.

"All right, Captain Red Eye!" Liza called. "Let's see whose ship is truly seaworthy, shall we?"

Using every bit of strength she possessed, Liza spun the wheel all the way to the right and held it there. The *Spirit* began to sail in a fast circle—and, thanks to the rope connecting the ships' bows, so did the *Befouler*.

Captain Red Eye roared again as his wheel spun out of control. The *Befouler* began sailing in a circle opposite the *Spirit*, like two dance partners twirling round and round. Between them, the murky waters began to churn faster and faster . . .

"It's working!" Peck cried, holding on to

the railing with one paw and the map with the other. "We're creating a whirlpool!"

"*Helllllp!*" Luglow went flying over the railing of the *Befouler,* landing in the water with a great splash. Two more Phantoms followed, and even Captain Red Eye had to grab on to a mast to keep from falling.

Liza's arms trembled with the effort of holding the *Spirit*'s wheel in place. She glanced back at the stern as Graham emerged from belowdecks, then called: "Cosmo! Get ready to untie the knot!"

"Ready when you are!" Cosmo clung to the bow, his paws on the knot.

Sir Gilbert stared at the center of the whirlpool, hoping the information Peck had gotten out of Captain Red Eye was accurate. If the *Befouler* couldn't actually open Phantom portals, this plan would surely fail . . .

Was it his imagination, or was the whirlpool changing from brown to purple? Sir Gilbert leaned as far over the railing as he dared, peering down into the depths. Dark purple swirling with green was glowing in the water now, and the tiger Alpha smiled. A Phantom portal was opening, growing wider by the second.

"On my count!" he cried, and everyone clung to the nearest railing or pole. "Three . . . two . . . one!"

Cosmo clipped the knot loose with his nails, and the *Spirit of Jamaa* broke free of the whirlpool. Captain Red Eye shook his tentacles menacingly as the *Befouler* was caught in the current, drifting closer and closer to the center—and the portal.

Gritting her teeth, Liza spun the *Spirit*'s wheel in the opposite direction. The current was strong, but she had faith that, thanks to Graham, their ship was stronger. The *Befouler* was halfway into the portal already. Just as the *Spirit* broke free of the current's pull—

"*Cosmo!*"

The koala Alpha's eyes were wide as he lost his grip on the bow. The other Alphas—Liza at the helm, Greely in the crow's nest, Sir Gilbert at the railing, and Graham at the stern—watched in horror, too far away to do anything as their friend began to fall toward the Phantom portal.

But Peck had noticed him losing his grip, and she hadn't wasted a second. She grabbed a hook secured to the mainsail's ropes and flung herself over the side of the ship.

"Gotcha!" Peck grabbed Cosmo's arm with her free paw, and the rope went taut. They dangled there, watching as the last of the *Befouler* was swallowed in the Phantom portal. Then something fluttered past them, and Peck gasped. "The map!"

"Grab it!" Cosmo squeaked, reaching for the map. But Peck didn't loosen her hold on her friend.

"Are you kidding?" she said with a shaky laugh. "Losing the map is okay. Losing you definitely isn't."

Cosmo grinned, and they watched as the map vanished into the portal, along with all the green slime and brown goop. The turquoise water stilled, and Peck heaved a sigh of relief.

"Peck! Cosmo!" Liza's worried face appeared over the railing, along with the other Alphas. Cosmo waved at them with his free arm.

"We're fine!" he called. "But would you mind pulling us up? This is pretty comfy, but I'd rather not sail all the way home this way!"

After Sir Gilbert and Greely pulled them to the deck safely, Cosmo gave Peck a big hug.

"Thanks," he said, eyes sparkling. "I know how much that map meant to you."

Peck blinked. "You didn't actually think I'd risk letting go of you just to save the map, did you?" She felt slightly ashamed when she thought about how important the map had been to her.

After everything the Alphas had just been through, the idea of buried treasure now seemed more silly than anything else.

"You *were* pretty fixated on it," Liza said with a kind smile. "But I was excited, too! Maps mean adventure, and that map certainly gave us one."

Cosmo nodded emphatically. "It gave me the opportunity to talk with those magnificent trees down in the caves."

"It gave us this ship!" Graham agreed, patting the *Spirit*'s railing lovingly.

"Not to mention," Greely added dryly, arching a brow at Peck, "it gave us the opportunity to see you in the most ridiculous pirate disguise of all time."

Everyone laughed at that. Sir Gilbert placed a paw on Peck's shoulder. "And most importantly," he told her, "the map led us here, which turned out to be exactly where we needed to be to once again save Jamaa from the Phantoms. I admit, I'd hoped the treasure might be a Heartstone or a clue as to where we might find Mira. Now I believe she left us that map knowing the Phantoms would bury their treasure here, and trusting we would find the map and set sail to intercept the *Befouler* when the time was right."

Peck beamed at her fellow Alphas. "You know what? I bet she did."

"Okay, enough chitchat, mateys!" Liza said, clapping her paws. "Hoist the sails! Swab the decks! Clean up this muck and goo! *Arr!*"

"*Arrr!*" the crew cried, still laughing as they returned to their posts. The Alphas smiled at one another, then set to work charting a new course for the *Spirit*.

Together, they set sail for home—and whatever new adventures waited for them in the exciting land of Jamaa.

CONTINUE YOUR ANIMAL JAM ADVENTURE!

The story continues online! Uncover this book's code to unlock a secret adventure on www.animaljam.com! Find the letters and numbers under stones at the beginning of each chapter, and put them together using the code below to unlock the secret password. Make sure to keep the letters and numbers in the right order of chapters one through ten!

Once you solve the code, go to www.animaljam.com/redeem or the Play Wild app to redeem your code!*

Replace	t	y	l	g	z	2
With	A	B	C	D	E	F
Replace	d	k	x	f	j	3
With	G	H	I	J	K	L
Replace	v	s	q	h	b	5
With	M	N	O	P	Q	R
Replace	4	a	c	r	p	w
With	S	T	U	V	W	X
Replace	i	n	e	m	o	u
With	Y	Z	1	2	3	4

*Each code valid for a one-time use.